LITTLE SIMON
An imprint of Simon & Schuster Children's Publishing Division
1230 Avenue of the Americas, New York, New York 10020
First Little Simon paperback edition February 2023
Copyright © 2023 by Simon & Schuster, Inc.
Also available in a Little Simon hardcover edition.
All rights reserved, including the right of reproduction in whole or in part in any form. LITTLE SIMON is a registered trademark of Simon & Schuster, Inc., and associated colophon is a trademark of Simon & Schuster, Inc.
For information about special discounts for bulk purchases, please contact Simon & Schuster Special Sales at 1-866-506-1949 or business@simonandschuster.com. The Simon & Schuster Speakers Bureau can bring authors to your live event. For more information or to book an event contact the Simon & Schuster Speakers Bureau at 1-866-248-3049 or visit our website at www.simonspeakers.com.
Designed by Leslie Mechanic
Manufactured in the United States of America 1222 LAK
10 9 8 7 6 5 4 3 2 1
Library of Congress Cataloging-in-Publication Data
Names: Higgins, Cam, author. | Landy, Ariel, illustrator.
Title: All you need is mud / by Cam Higgins ; illustrated by Ariel Landy.
| Description: First Little Simon edition. | New York : Little Simon, 2023.
| Series: Good dog ; 10 | Audience: Ages 5–9. | Summary: Bo and his pig pal Zonk play in the mud together, but when Zonk's pet rock Rocky gets chipped and Zonk is upset, Bo must learn how to be a good, supportive friend to Zonk. | Identifiers: LCCN 2022031493 (print) | LCCN 2022031494 (ebook) | ISBN 9781665930697 (paperback) | ISBN 9781665930703 (hardcover) | ISBN 9781665930710 (ebook) | Subjects: CYAC: Dogs—Fiction. | Animals—Infancy—Fiction. | Pigs—Fiction. | Best friends—Fiction. | Friendship—Fiction. | Classification: LCC PZ7.1.H54497 All 2023 (print) | LCC PZ7.1.H54497 (ebook) | DDC [Fic]—dc23
LC record available at https://lccn.loc.gov/2022031493

GOOD D🐾G 10

All You Need Is Mud

by
Cam Higgins

illustrated by
Ariel Landy

LITTLE SIMON

New York London Toronto Sydney New Delhi

CONTENTS

Meet Rocky

My name is Bo, and you need to know something about me.

I totally love springtime at the Davis farm!

The sweet smell of freshly cut grass, the sun shining overhead, and brand-new flowers everywhere, waiting to be dug up.

But after a spring rain, there's only one place to find me—running through the field.

Why? Because all that grass is covered with tiny drops of water that keep me cool.

So, of course, it all started with a dash through the field. My tongue and ears flapped in the breeze. Everything was perfect. Until I reached the barn.

Two small shadows were waiting in the doorway. It was King and Diva, the barn cats.

"Why does that pup keep running through the fields making such a racket?" King asked.

"Bo the bumbler *is* such a bother!" Diva agreed. "And the smell of wet puppy is so very yucky."

"I heard even the skunks think he stinks," said King. "Pee-yew!"

In case you don't know, cats and dogs don't always get along. Me and the barn cats, though, well, we almost never got along.

"Sorry, King and Diva," I called out. "You grumps can't get me down today!"

I raced by them and went to see Zonks, my piggy pal. He was in his pigpen, enjoying the wet, squishy mud.

"Hi, Bo!" he called. "Come on in! The mud feels great!"

"Thanks, Zonks," I said. "I was going to run through the field again. Do you want to join me?"

"Who wants to run when you can roll?" said Zonks as he flopped back into the mud.

That pig had a point. There was nothing like a roll in the mud. But I knew that mud would still be muddy later. Wet grass, on the other paw, would dry out in the sun soon.

"I'll be back in a flash, Zonks," I told him.

"Okay," said Zonks. "But there *is* something I want to show you, so make sure to swing by!"

Something to show me? Now I was interested. What could it be?

I looked at the field, and then I looked back at Zonks. The field would have to wait. My friend had a surprise.

So I said, "I guess I could spare a minute or two, if you want to show me what it is."

"Yay!" Zonks cheered.

Then he started sniffing around in the mud.

"Um, what are you doing?" I asked.

"Oh, I buried it for safekeeping because it is *so cool*," he explained.

"Do you want some help?" I asked. "I am very good at digging."

"Sure! Dig here," Zonks said.

I bounced to the spot by Zonks and dug with my front paws. The cold mud felt wonderful between my toes. "Aha! You found it!" Zonks called out.

I stopped digging and stepped back to let Zonks reach in and find his so cool thing.

Then he turned around and held up . . . a rock.

"It's a rock?" I asked.

I did not know why a rock was cool or special. Rocks are everywhere around here.

"It's not any old rock," Zonks said happily. "Bo, meet my pet rock, Rocky!"

Rocky was a small, gray rock with a dent on one side that sort of made a smiley face. I gave it a sniff, because that's how dogs meet other friends. Rocky smelled muddy and a little like Zonks.

That pig looked so proud of Rocky, but Rocky just looked like a rock to me. I could find rocks just like this one all around the farm.

"Don't you think he's great?" Zonks asked.

"Um, yeah, sure," I said. "If you say so."

"What do you mean?" Zonks cried.
"Why aren't you more excited to
meet Rocky? He's my pet!"

Let me tell you, I had no idea what to tell Zonks. But luckily, I didn't have to say anything because a flash of gray fur on the top of the fence caught my eye.

"SQUIRREL!" I roared.

The Pig's
Not All Right

Here's a tip: if you ever need to make a quick escape, just yell "SQUIRREL!" and run.

Believe me, it works for dogs all the time.

And since I didn't want to hurt Zonks's feelings about Rocky, I took off after that squirrel.

The chase went all around the pigpen, and mud splattered everywhere—my fur, the fence—I mean *everywhere*.

As I was running in circles, I kicked something hard with my paw and heard it smack against the fence. But that squirrel did not slow down, which meant I didn't slow down either.

Then, out of the corner of my eye,
I spotted Zonks rolling something
with his foot.

"Oh, no, you're chipped!" he said.

But I could not stop. I would not stop!

The squirrel finally leaped off the fence and darted out into the field.

"That's right, you better run!" I called after him. "No squirrels allowed in my best buddy's pigpen!"

I turned back to Zonks, but he looked really sad.

"Don't worry. That squirrel won't
show his face around here anymore,"
I promised.

But that didn't make Zonks smile.
Not at all. Instead he was mumbling
to something on the ground.

That's when my human siblings, Imani and Wyatt, came over. They were doing their morning chores, but they stopped by Zonks's fence.

"Gosh, how did you manage to get the fence so dirty again, Zonks?" Imani asked sweetly. Her voice matched the smile on her face, but Zonks kept looking down at the ground.

Then Wyatt looked at me. "Let me guess. You invited Bo over, and he saw a squirrel."

Yeah, my human brother and sister know me well. I gave them a bark to say, "That's right!"

But Zonks was not as excited as I was. He had a strange look on his face. I wondered what was going on.

"Well, pigs will be pigs, and pups will be pups," said Wyatt. "And someone is getting a bath tonight, Bo."

As they walked away to continue their farm tasks, I gave Zonks a big puppy smile. Being messy was one of the best things ever. Even Imani and Wyatt knew that . . . kind of.

But Zonks did not smile back.

I jogged toward him and asked,
"Hey, what's going on? Why aren't
you playing in the mud?"

He still didn't answer.

"Zonks?" I said. "Oh, no, do you have mud in your ears? I hate it when that happens."

Zonks finally turned around. He looked very sad.

"Here," he said softly. He showed his rock to me. "Look at Rocky."

I looked, but I didn't see anything. It just looked like a regular old rock to me.

"Oh, sorry, uh, hi, Rocky," I said. "Did you have fun at the squirrel chase?"

"No, he did not!" Zonks snapped. "He's chipped, Bo. Right there, on the corner."

I squinted and looked harder. There was a tiny chip on Zonks's rock. It was so teeny tiny, though, that you could hardly see it unless you looked at it really, really close.

But that didn't matter to Zonks. He was clearly upset.

Luckily, I am a puppy with bright ideas. And I knew just the thing to cheer him up!

"It's okay, Zonks. I can help—we'll go find you another rock!" I said. "There are loads of them right outside your pen!"

No Rock
Like Rocky

Zonks looked surprised.

"What?" he oinked. "I don't want another rock. You can't just find a new pet rock. I can't just replace Rocky!"

I tilted my head and gave a surprised woof, because this was news to me.

35

"Bo, you're one of my best friends," Zonks said. "Even if we're different kinds of animals, we always love doing the same things, like playing in the mud, lying in the sunshine, and eating together. And all that is amazing."

"Definitely!" I barked.

"But I don't think you understand me right now. Rocky is special to me," Zonks explained. "It took me ages to find him—the most perfect pet rock. I don't want to replace him."

"It's just a rock, though," I said. "It isn't like Rocky is a delicious bone or a wonderful toy that you can't replace.

It's always easy to find a different rock. You could throw a rock around here, and you'd probably hit *another* rock!"

"Bo! I don't want to find another rock!" Zonks oinked. "And I think I would like to be alone right now."

Then he spun around and turned his curly pink tail to me.

I watched Zonks leave the pigpen
and wondered what I had done
wrong.

Suddenly I heard a clucking. You
guessed it. It was Clucks.

"Bo, I couldn't help overhearing you and Zonks," she said. "I really must tell you, that wasn't very nice. You need to give Zonks some space."

"I don't understand!" I woofed. "I'm trying to be a good friend to Zonks. I just know that a new rock will help him feel better."

"Bo, that is not what Zonks needs right now," Clucks clucked.

"What do you mean?" I asked. "A shiny rock with no dents will cheer him up. He just doesn't know it yet!"

Clucks just shook her feathery head and cluck, cluck, clucked. Then she walked away.

Once again, it was up to me to save the day. I was a pup with a mission! I set off to find a new rock for Zonks.

I was positive that if I found the right rock, my friend would feel better.

I began digging in the yard, and soon enough, I had found a whole bunch of rocks, all gray and round like Rocky.

These will work great, I thought.

I picked up the rocks in my mouth and went to find Zonks.

Pick a Rock, Any Rock

I zipped over to the barn, excited to show Zonks the rocks I'd found. Luckily, he was back inside his pen. Carefully, I dropped the rocks in front of him.

"Look, Zonks!" I cheered. "I'm sorry about Rocky, so I found you some new rocks. One of these will definitely make a perfect pet rock."

I scooted some around with my nose and pushed one forward. "I think this one might be even better than Rocky!"

Zonks huffed at that. "Bo, I already told you, none of these rocks can replace Rocky! I can't believe you thought it would be so easy!"

I didn't know what to say. My friend
had gone from sad to mad.

"You know what?" he said. "I'm
leaving. Again! And don't follow me
this time!"

Zonks waddled away, and I let out a
little whine. Because if he was feeling
sad, then mad . . . I was feeling bad.

I had never seen Zonks act like this. Were we in a . . . fight?

"Well, if you're going to leave, then I'm going to leave too!" I yelled at him. "And don't follow me, either, because I'm going to . . . to . . . to a no-pig place!"

"SNORT!" was the only thing Zonks said. Then he turned the corner and was gone.

I didn't know what was going on with him. But now I had to figure out why pigs were so hard to understand.

And if Zonks wouldn't tell me what was wrong, maybe another friend would.

It was time to talk to Comet.

5

A Horse in Deed

Comet was also in the barn, which Wyatt and Imani had just swept and tidied as part of their daily chores. Comet always liked her stable to be neat and clean.

"Hello, Comet," I called.

She was munching on some hay. Just seeing her made me feel better.

Comet always put me in a good mood. That's what friends are supposed to do, right?

"Hi, Bo," she said. "Hey, what's wrong? Is something bothering you?"

Comet could tell just by looking at me that I was feeling down. Good buddies always know when something isn't right.

"Well, something happened with Zonks today," I began.

Comet listened as I described the morning, from Zonks getting all quiet after I chased the squirrel, to his turning his back to me, to his shouting about not wanting a new rock, and walking away from me again.

When I had finished, I felt like a big rock had been lifted off my chest.

Comet had not spoken a word since I began my tale of piggy woe.

Then she said thoughtfully, "I see."

"Phew!" I said. "I'm glad somebody knows what's going on. Now can you tell me?"

Comet stamped her hoof and continued, "Maybe what Zonks wants is not a replacement for his rock, but something else."

"I don't know what you mean," I whined.

"Well, what if you try to think about how Zonks might be feeling now? Maybe then you'll find an answer," Comet suggested.

Think about how Zonks is feeling? What about how I am feeling? I thought.

"Okay, thanks," I replied, more confused than ever. "I'll see you later, Comet."

Horses are beautiful creatures, but sometimes they are mysterious. I wasn't sure what a rock had to do with feelings, but I knew one thing: I had a lot of thinking to do.

Rocks on the Mind

I wandered out of the barn and deep into my own thoughts.

Maybe that's why I wasn't watching where I was going and suddenly heard a loud squawk.

Oops! I had bumped into Clucks and Rufus.

"I'm so sorry," I said. "Excuse me!"

"That's okay, Bo," said Clucks. "How are you doing?"

"You know what—not great!" I said. "For the first time ever, in the history of Zonks and me being friends, I have no idea what a pig wants or what he feels. Pigs are harder to understand than I thought!"

"Really, Bo, it doesn't seem that hard to me!" Clucks clucked loudly. "You are thinking about yourself and not your friend. You chipped Zonks's rock! And you hurt his feelings! Don't you see that?"

I tilted my head and stared at her.

"You should apologize to Zonks," she added. "This is clearly your fault."

My fault? I didn't like the sound of that. I mean, I didn't even really know what I had done wrong.

A bad, itchy feeling washed all over my body. I didn't like it one bit!

Suddenly, Rufus stepped forward.
He was a wise rooster, and when he
talked, all the animals listened. Usually
because he's telling us to wake up!

Rufus shook out his feathers, puffed his chest, and said, "Well, it seems to me that this young pup means well. He was only trying to help the pig find a new pet rock. If you ask me, I think Zonks is being a little selfish!"

Clucks looked at the rooster and flapped her wings.

"No one asked you!" she said.

Then she strutted away, pecking at the ground as she went.

Oh, no, what had I started?

A
Barnyard Mess

Before I knew it, all the other animals on the Davis farm had heard about what was going on.

The sheep baaed about how Zonks and I were mad at each other. The chicks cheeped about it, and they began to argue among themselves over who was right—Zonks or me.

Then Diva and King stalked over, and even they couldn't agree. King began to hiss in the direction of Zonks's pigpen, while Diva hissed at me.

"Pup versus pig! Of course the pig is right," Diva spat. "That silly little pup never gets it right."

"For once, I'm going to take young Bo's side," King said. Then he narrowed his golden eyes at Diva and smiled a sneaky grin.

Were the cats just choosing sides because they knew it would stir up a big old cat fight?

Soon, even more animals were fussing about who was right and who was wrong. All the animals had picked a side. Some said they were Team Bo. Others said they were Team Zonks.

Helplessly, I stood and watched as the arguing grew louder. The itchy feeling was getting worse. Now the pads of my paws were feeling itchy as well.

I needed to do something. None of this was helping. There was only one animal I needed to talk to.

Without a word to any of the others, I slipped away and headed toward Zonks's pen.

He was still there, lying in the mud.
But he wasn't rolling around in it.

"Zonks?" I said softly.

"What do you want?" he asked
without looking at me.

I stepped closer. "Can we talk?"

"Why should we, when you don't even care that it was you who made a mess inside my pen?" Zonks said.

Mess? We loved making messes together—that was how we first became friends, getting messy in the mud. When had making a mess in the pigpen become a bad thing?

It didn't seem like Zonks felt ready to talk to me. I bowed my head and left his pen without another word. How had we gotten into such a bad fight?

Misss–
Communication

When I left the pen, I was hoping to find someplace quiet. But the barnyard was blathering!

So I trotted into the field . . . but guess who was waiting for me there. It was the last two animals I ever thought I'd find in the wet grass: King and Diva.

"Bo, we would like to help solve this terrible problem you and Zonks are having," King said.

"Yesss, we always want to help," Diva added with a slight hiss.

"Um, okay," I said. "Well, could you please tell Zonks that I would like to help him feel better by finding him a new rock?"

"Of course," said Diva. "Come with us!"

Now, if a cat ever says, "Come with us," here's a tip: don't go with them.

I wish someone had told me that earlier, because I followed them back to the pigpen, and it did not go well.

"Zonks," King said through the fence, "Bo thinks your old rock stinks."

"Tell Bo that Rocky does not smell bad!" Zonks oinked angrily.

"Bo, Zonks thinks you smell bad," Diva reported.

What? I turned to sniff around my front leg. I didn't smell anything.

"Well, can you please tell Zonks that I think he just needs to go and find a new rock?" I said.

"Zonks, Bo wants you and Rocky to go . . . away . . . forever," King said with an evil cat smile.

"Ugh! That was not what I said at all, and you know it!" I barked at the cats, but they just hissed with laughter.

Now Zonks stomped off, and I stomped off in a different direction.

I headed toward the field because I had wanted to run through the field all morning. Maybe it would still be wet.

But just before I got there, I came to a sudden stop. What good was running through a field if your friend was mad at you?

So I went back to make things right.

This time Zonks wasn't in the pigpen. And he wasn't in the barn.

Then I heard a trotting sound and called out.

"Zonks! Zonks! Is that you?" I asked.

But it wasn't Zonks. It was a large horse named Star. Star was Comet's mom, and she could be very funny.

"I should hope I don't sound like a pig," Star said with a laugh.

"Sorry, I was looking for Zonks," I told her.

"Ah, yes, I've heard you and Zonks had quite a day together," said Star.

"Yes, ma'am," I agreed, because it was true.

"Well, Zonks is out with Nanny Sheep," Star said. "I think they were going to run through the field."

Run through the field! I thought. I wanted to run through the field with Zonks, and he said no. Now he was running through the field with someone else? Oh, I was getting angry.

"Thanks, Star," I said. "I'll see if I can catch up with them."

It didn't take long to spot Nanny Sheep's white fluff in the field, so I raced in that direction. And when I got there, what do you think I found?

Nanny Sheep was standing with
Zonks . . . next to a mud puddle . . .
in the middle of the wet field!
What?!

As I drew nearer, I hid and listened.

Zonks said, "Look, Nanny Sheep. It's our very own fresh mud puddle! Rolling in the mud is so much fun, I promise. Getting all muddy is the best. It feels really good. Seriously! Try it!"

Was Zonks looking for a new mud-rolling buddy? But that was our thing! Was he replacing me? Did he not want to be friends anymore? All over a silly rock?

Luckily, Nanny Sheep had no interest in getting dirty.

"This is a job for a pig and a dog," she said. "Where is Bo anyway?"

"I don't know and I don't care," said Zonks. "And if you're not getting in the mud, I might as well go home."

Nanny tried to stop him, but Zonks walked away. Then I snuck over to Nanny Sheep.

"Oh, there you are, pup," she said. "It seems your friend needs you."

"Really?" I asked. "Because it seems like we're not even friends anymore. Do you think you could help me try to understand how Zonks might be feeling?"

Nanny Sheep smiled. "Yes, of course, Bo. I don't like seeing you and Zonks this way. Now tell me, how can I help?"

9

A Little Help from a Friend

"I don't know where to start," I told Nanny Sheep.

"Why don't you start at the beginning?" she said.

"Okay," I began. "Well, I was going to run through the fields, and then Zonks had something to show me. It was his new pet rock, Rocky.

Then a squirrel showed up, and I mean, squirrels can't just expect to sit on the fences and think it's okay. So I chased him all around. They have to know that I'm on to them! And I maybe, definitely kicked Rocky, and he got chipped. But it was an accident. And besides, it's just a plain old rock!"

"Hmm," said Nanny Sheep. "I know you didn't mean to chip Rocky. But can you imagine how you would feel if Rocky was your bone, and your bone got broken, and Zonks thought he could replace it with some other old bone?"

"Huh," I woofed. "I guess that would make me pretty upset. Because my bone is my bone. I think I get it now. But what about how Diva said that Zonks said I smell? That wasn't the way friends talk to each other."

"Oh, you know those two barn cats like to stir up trouble," Nanny Sheep said with a giggle. "I don't think that's what Zonks really said."

"Right," I said. That made sense.
"But what about when I saw you and
Zonks rolling in the mud together?
That made me feel kind of bad too.
Like he wanted to replace me."

"Zonks could never replace you," said Nanny Sheep. "Think about it. What other animal on this farm would want to roll around in the mud?"

I thought about that and didn't have a good answer. Mud was almost always a pup-and-pig adventure.

I knew what I had to do. "Nanny Sheep, I'm ready to talk to Zonks."

All You Need Is Mud

I followed Nanny Sheep over to the pigpen. She needed to be there because it's hard to be mad when Nanny Sheep is around.

"Zonks," Nanny Sheep called out. "Bo would like to talk to you."

"Okay," the pig oinked, looking a bit confused as he walked over.

"Zonks, I'm sorry," I began. "I'm sorry I made a mess in your pen, and I'm sorry I didn't understand how special Rocky is to you. And I'm really sorry I chipped him."

"Thanks, Bo," Zonks said. "I'm glad you understand why I was upset that you chipped Rocky . . . and why I could never just replace him."

"Oh, I totally understand now, thanks to Nanny Sheep," I woofed. "Plus, Rocky is really cute. I think he makes a great pet rock."

"He sure does," Zonks oinked.

"Having a pet rock to take care of must be fun," I said.

"I'm glad you think so," said Zonks. "Because I have another surprise for you."

"For me?" I barked excitedly. "What could it be?"

Zonks smiled a big pig smile. "Well, there was a reason I went out into the field with Nanny Sheep. I wanted to find this for you."

He stretched out his piggy arms, and I looked down. Zonks was holding a smooth rock with dents that looked like eyes and a mouth!

"It's for you, Bo," said Zonks. "Your own pet rock! Do you like it?"

"Like it?" I said. "I LOVE IT! In fact, I'd say that it ROCKS!"

That made Zonks squeal with laughter. Oh, how I had missed that sound.

"Now you need to name it," Zonks said.

I stared at the rock and thought as hard as a puppy could. Then I knew there was only one name that would work.

"Attention, everyone," I called out. "I would like you to meet . . . *Rockefeller*. Maybe he and Rocky can be friends!"

"Oh, Rockefeller yeah!" Zonks oinked excitedly. "Best friends!"

"Thanks, Zonks," I said. "I don't have nearly as much fun when you're mad at me!"

"I don't have as much fun when I'm mad at you either!" Zonks said.

"Hey," I said. "Why don't we take Rocky and Rockefeller out to that perfect mud puddle in the field for a good ol' game of roll-in-the-mud?"

"I thought you'd never ask!" Zonks said.

"I will sit this one out, but I'll watch you two play," Nanny Sheep baaed happily.

As we ran to the field, I thought, *Sometimes, all you need is mud.*

And good friends—no matter if they're rocks or pups or pigs.

Sit. Stay. Read.

Here are more GOOD DOG adventures!

GOOD D🐾G 1

Home Is Where the Heart Is

GOOD D🐾G 2

Raised in a Barn

GOOD D🐾G 3

Herd You Loud and Clear

GOOD D🐾G 4

Fireworks Night

GOOD D🐾G 5

The Swimming Hole

GOOD D🐾G 6

Life Is Good

GOOD D🐾G 7

Barnyard Buddies

GOOD D🐾G 8

Puppy Luck

GOOD D🐾G 9

Sweater Weather